Helping families cope with paternal separation

For Ben and Ellie, with much love from Daddy
C.M.

For you, Dad, with love always
E.Y.

MY DADDY'S GOING AWAY
A PICTURE CORGI BOOK 978 0 552 56725 1

First published in Great Britain in 2009 by Giddy Mangoes Limited.
This edition with new illustrations published in Great Britain in 2013 by Doubleday,
an imprint of Random House Children's Publishers UK
A Random House Group Company

Doubleday edition published 2013
Picture Corgi edition published 2014

10 9 8 7 6 5 4 3 2 1

HRH The Prince of Wales photograph by kind permission of Mario Testino.

Picture Corgi Books are published by RANDOM HOUSE CHILDREN'S PUBLISHERS UK
61–63 Uxbridge Road, London W5 5SA

www.**randomhousechildrens**.co.uk
www.**randomhouse**.co.uk
www.mydaddysgoingaway.com

Addresses for companies within The Random House Group Limited can be found at:
www.randomhouse.co.uk/offices.htm
THE RANDOM HOUSE GROUP Limited Reg. No. 954009
A CIP catalogue record for this book is available from the British Library.
Printed in China

The Random House Group Limited supports the Forest Stewardship Council® (FSC®), the leading international forest-certification organisation. Our books carrying the FSC label are printed on FSC®-certified paper. FSC is the only forest-certification scheme supported by the leading environmental organisations, including Greenpeace. Our paper procurement policy can be found at www.randomhouse.co.uk/environment.

My Daddy's Going Away

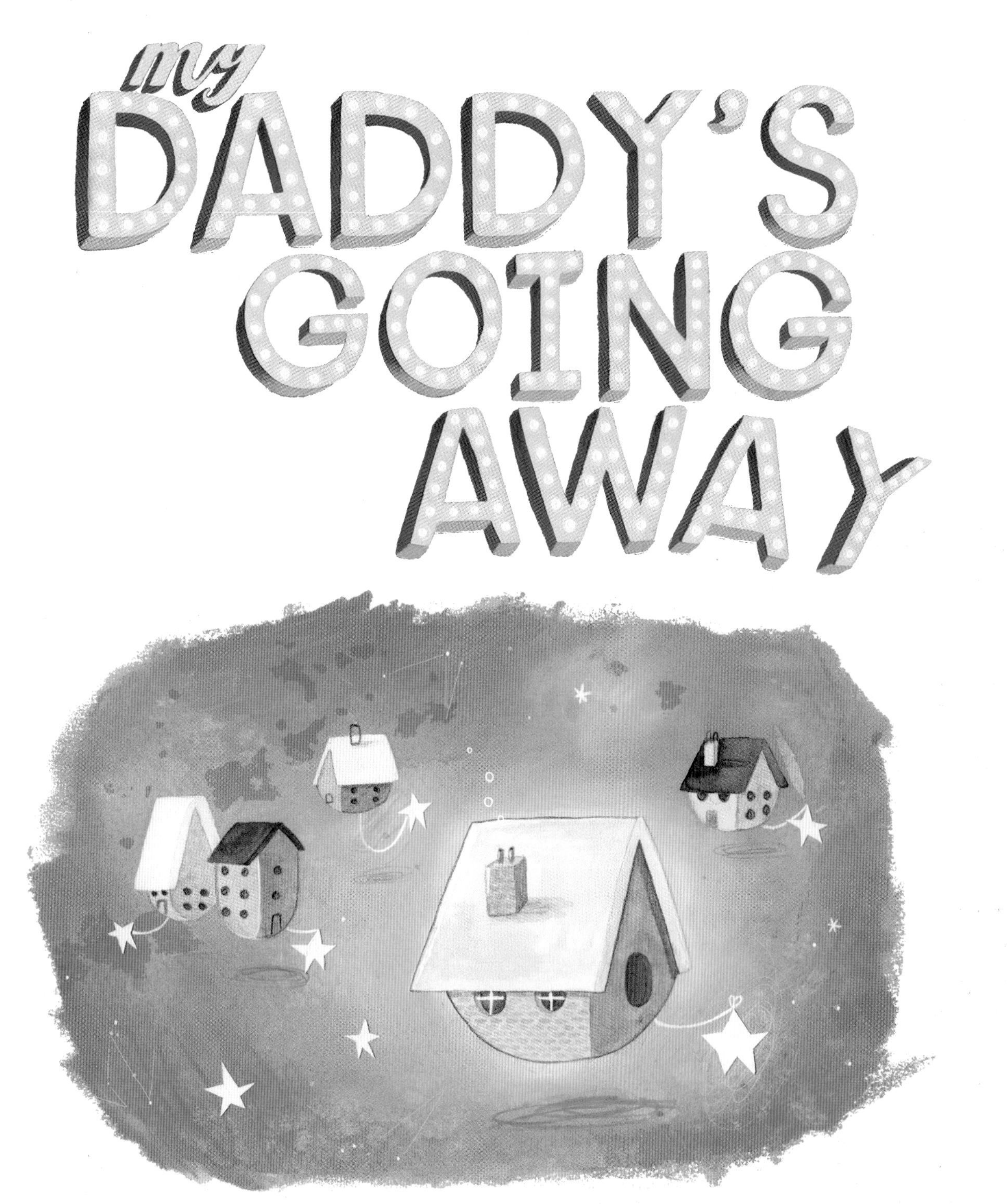

CHRISTOPHER MACGREGOR AND EMMA YARLETT

PICTURE CORGI

CLARENCE HOUSE

I am delighted to introduce this charming book; it not only promotes Combat Stress of which I am Patron, but thoughtfully prepares young children and their families to cope with the challenges of temporary paternal separation. As a father, I can only too well understand the strains on family wellbeing that absence can bring. Within this book, each cheerful illustration complements an insightful verse that, on many levels, can be used within your community or family to strengthen bonds and develop coping strategies. 'My Daddy's Going Away…' should really be read by all families.

Charles

My Daddy's going away, you know,
He says it's for a while.

Spaghetti's almost knitted!

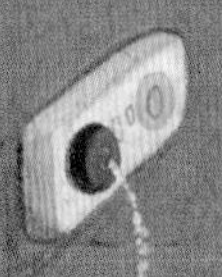

We'll miss our hugs and storytime,
We'll miss his funny **SmiLe**.

My Mummy says he'll be back soon
And only time will tell
How long it takes in far-off lands
For his socks to really **SMELL!**

There's lots to do before he goes,
We already want him back,

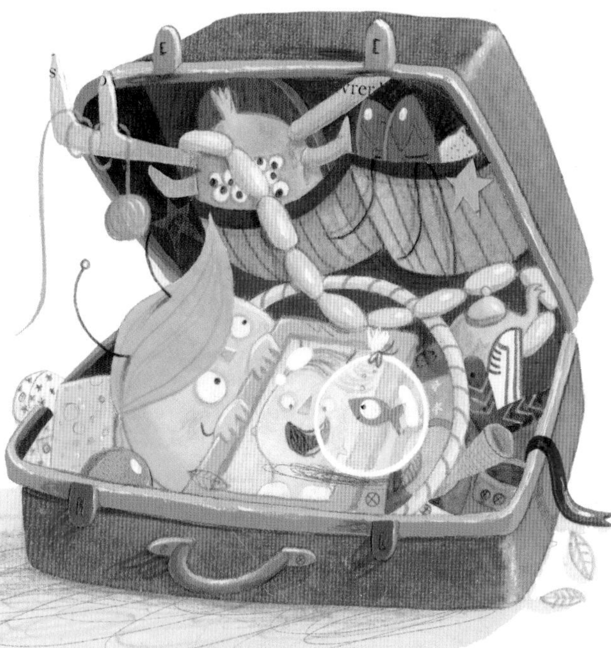

But he hasn't even left us yet,
So we're helping him to pack.

We give him gifts to show our LOVe,
And now he has to fly,

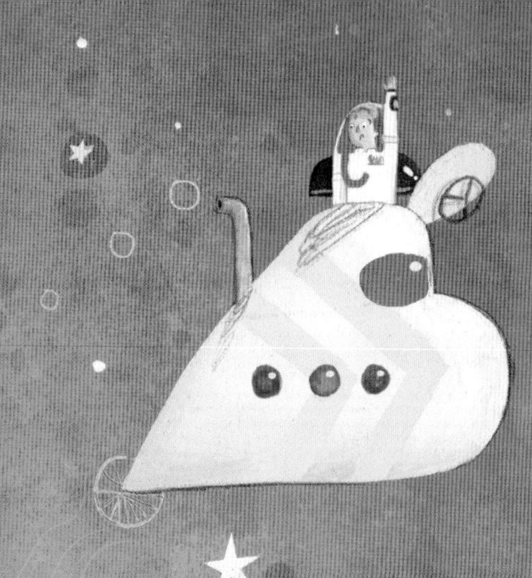

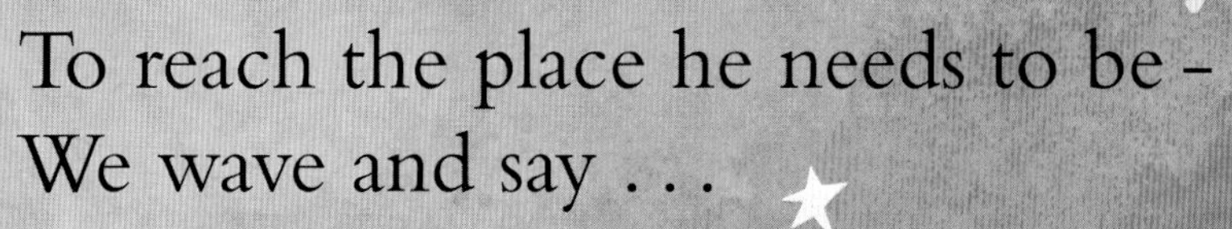

To reach the place he needs to be -
We wave and say . . .

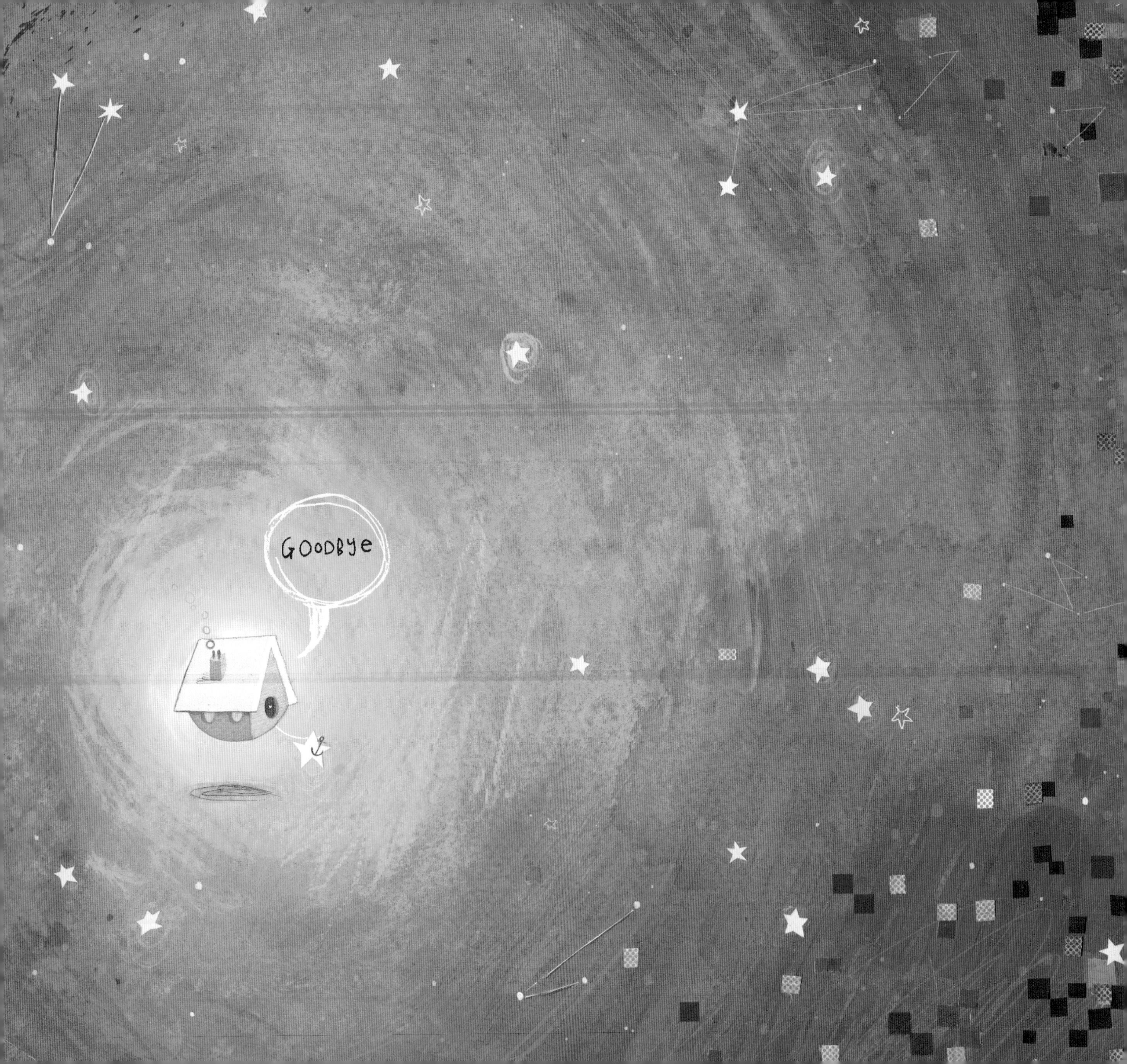
GOODBYE

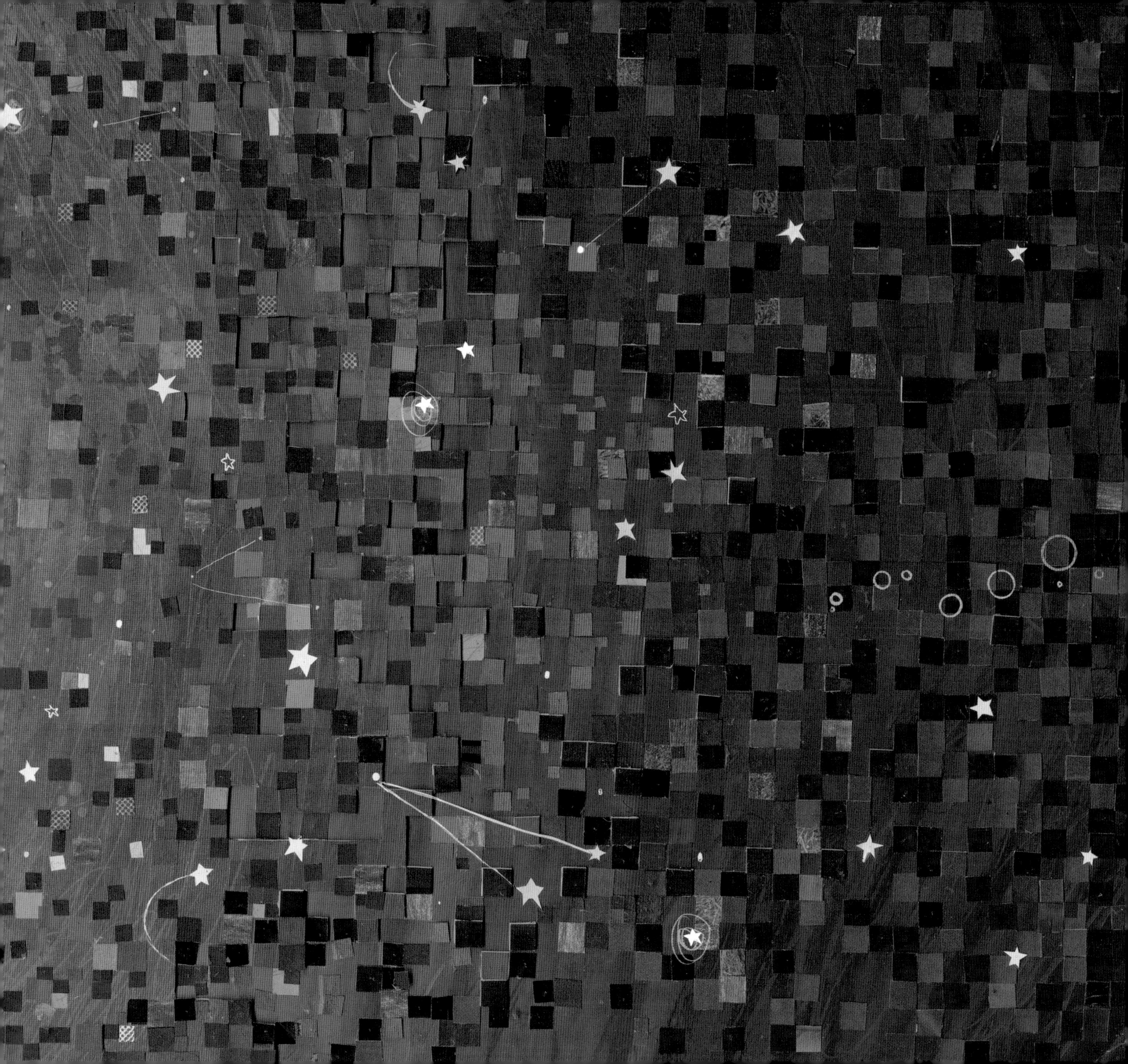

My Daddy's gone away, you know.
He said he'd rather stay,
But other people need him too
On each and every day.

He's working hard to conquer all
That comes into his path,

But I wish he was at home with me
Putting bubbles in my bath!

To reach out far and say hello,
I've sent a slow-coach letter.

We've made him films, sent parcels too,
But chatting's so much better.

My Daddy sends us
things he's found,
And getting post is cool,

But best of all I like it when
I can show things off at school.

If the sun gives way to cloud

And I'm not sure
why he's gone,

I'll talk to Mum
and my best friend,

And that will make me . . .

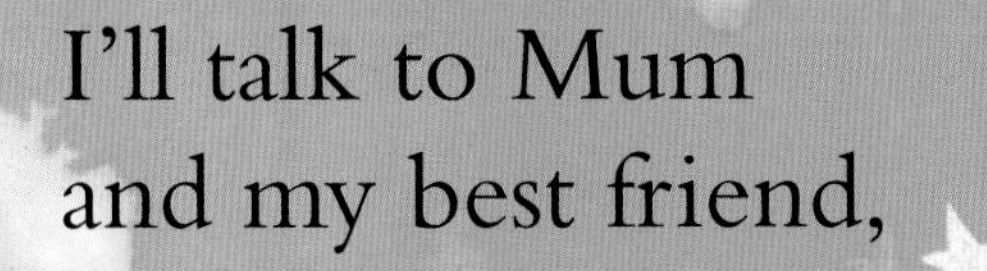

I know he loves me more each day
Our separation grows,

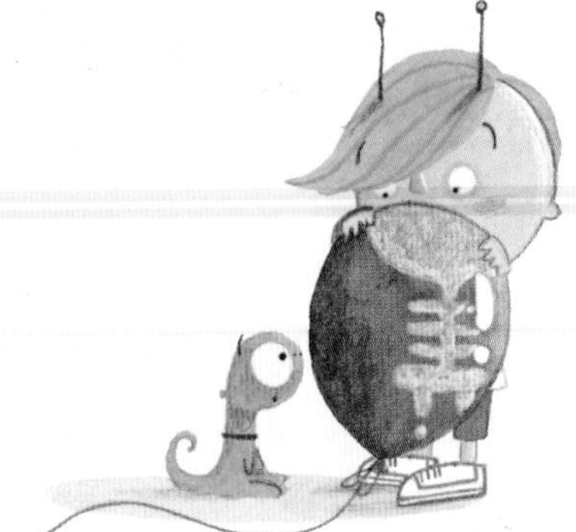

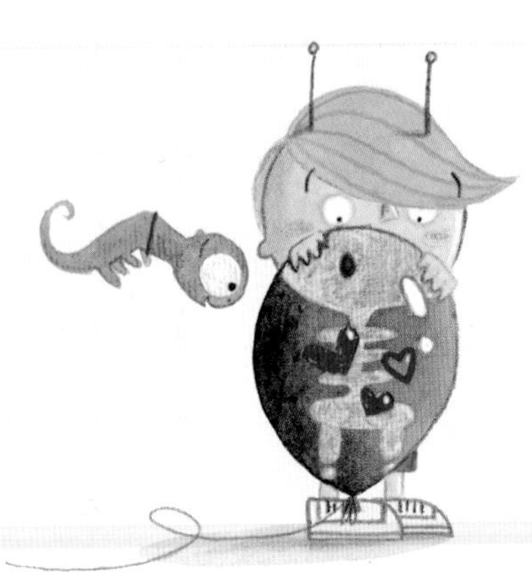

It's hard enough to squeeze it all
Between my head and toes.

POP!

At night before he goes to sleep, Daddy says a little prayer.

Sometimes I think
I hear it come and . . .
WHISPER
in the air.

We miss each other most of all
As we snuggle in our beds,

But we share the same warm blanket
Of STARS above our heads.

I'll dream of how we'll spend our time
In warm and wacky ways,
Then colour in a calendar
To count the missing days.

When Dad comes home we'll go on trips,
Fly kites, and camping too,
Explore the world of dinosaurs
And see tigers at the zoo.

YARLETT'S
ROOF GARDEN
Mooring STAR
APPRENTICESHIPS *
WORLD of DINOSAURS
TAXI
SPACEBOAT RIDES

e eEeeEE
DADDy

My Daddy's coming home, you know,
And we can hardly wait!
We'll hang balloons and jump up high!
We'll make a chocolate cake!

My Daddy's coming home today!
I can't believe it's true.

A hug is worth
a thousand words –

My kiss just . . .

I LOVE YOU!

My Daddy's Going Away supports the work of Combat Stress

Combat Stress is a charity that looks after people who have left the Armed Forces but who have, unfortunately, been deeply upset by some of the experiences they have had while serving.

Few of us know how we would react to being in a war zone, conflict or humanitarian disaster. Few of us will ever be called upon to witness these things, but for those who do, proper care and support must be available – and fortunately, with the help of Combat Stress, it is. For almost a hundred years Combat Stress has provided a unique lifeline to Veterans suffering psychological trauma as a result of their Service careers.

There is a clear need for Combat Stress's unique support – the charity has seen a huge increase in referrals in recent times. Combat Stress is there – long after the war has ended – for those Veterans whose battles continue.

Please visit www.**combatstress**.org.uk for further information.

Combat Stress is a Registered Charity: England & Wales No. 206002; Scotland No. SC 038828 / Company Limited by Guarantee No. 256353.

* * *

For ideas, support and fun things to do, as well as to find out more about Christopher MacGregor's inspiration and the true story behind this book, please visit www.**mydaddysgoingaway**.com

Coming soon: *My Mummy's Going Away*

The END